# Summer Spirits

### Book One

by Kelly A. Yang

ISBN-13:
978-1533503169

ISBN-10:
1533503168

# DEDICATION

I would like to dedicate this book to all the supporters, teachers and mentors who have helped me so far in my life. Without them, this book would not have been possible. ☺

# TABLE OF CONTENTS

## Part I: Stacy

## Part II: Lizzy

# PART I: STACY

## CHAPTER 1:
### The Last Day of Fifth Grade

Splash!

I flipped and dove into the water, swimming to the pool's ledge. Twisting around, I waited for my best friend, Tasha, to jump off the diving board. She performed a somersault and crashed into the water, her red hair flying behind her. We got out of the pool and dried off.

Looking around, I tried to find the patio, in pursuit of some snacks. Walking around the pool, we headed towards the play structure. To the left, I saw some juniper trees blocking the view of another area. In this huge backyard, anything could be anywhere! We found our way around the junipers and saw the patio. Someone had placed a bowl filled with granola bars on a picnic table.

We quickly grabbed some and went to see what to do next.

Today was the last day of 5th grade, and the entire grade was celebrating at a pool party. We had just completed the diving contest. Adam Jones won the contest with a super high, twist jump, followed by a somersault. He was celebrating with his friends, lying on the grass and eating snacks. Tasha and I walked towards the grass and saw our other friends, Megan and Hazel, wave us over.

"Stacy, Tasha! Come over here!" Megan called. We gave wide berth to Adam and his gang and raced over to Megan and Hazel. Adam was the ringleader of his group of goons. They were considered bullies, always playing practical jokes on unsuspecting victims.

"Everyone, please gather around. The next activity is the scavenger hunt," our teacher, Ms. Starr, announced.

"Do you wanna be in our group?" Hazel asked.

"Sure! Yeah!" Tasha and I chorused excitedly.

We made our way over to the rest of the grade, where the teacher was explaining the rules.

"No pushing or shoving - there will be plenty of clues for everyone," Ms. Starr was saying.

"Please get into groups of four, and I will give you the first clue."

Tasha, Megan, Hazel, and I automatically linked arms.

"Now, mind you, there might be some clues in the pool too."
Questions broke out like bees from a hive.

"How-?"

"In the pool-?"

Everyone was talking, and Ms. Starr was smiling.

"Yes class," she said, getting everyone's attention.

"There will be some clues in the pool. There is one clue for every group, so don't worry if you are not there first."

With that, she handed out the first clue, and the scavenger hunt began.

# CHAPTER 2:
## The Scavenger Hunt

Megan, Tasha, and Hazel gathered around me as we read the first clue.

*"High in a place where the birds like to sit,"* Hazel read out loud.

"Trees!" Tasha exclaimed.

We ran toward the nearest tree and looked skyward. We did see some birds, but they were too far up in the tree to reach.

"What are we going to do?" asked Megan. "Are we supposed to climb way up there?"

With that, she grabbed the nearest branch and hoisted herself up. She kept repeating the process until there were no more strong tree limbs. Standing on the last sturdy branch, she looked up and grabbed the next one. She tested it and put some of her weight on it.

*Snap!* It cracked in half and fell to the ground.

"Megan! Why don't you come down?" I shouted.

"I am trying to figure out how!" she screamed.

"Do you want me to get some help?"

"Nope! I think I've got it!"

She lowered herself down to one branch and then repeated the process until she was about 5 feet off the ground. Then, she jumped. Brushing dirt off her shirt, she said, "Let's have another look at that clue."

We gathered around Hazel again as she read the clue.

*'High in a place where the birds like to sit.'*

"Hmm, birds also like to sit... where?" Megan asked.

Hazel quickly scanned the backyard, her eyes landing on the fence that was covered with bird droppings.

"The fence!" she cried.

However, in this enormous area, which part of the fence? Fences surrounded the entire backyard, so the clue could be anywhere!

We dashed over to the nearest area of fence, but it was semi-covered by trees. Megan squirmed around the tree; and, sure enough, another clue was waiting for us. There was a tube of sunscreen, but further down, I could see a second tube.

"*They must be spread out on the fence because it covers the whole perimeter of the backyard,*" I thought. "*Oh, that's smart; that way, other groups can't see each other getting the clue.*"

We put the sunscreen in the bag that Ms. Starr had given every group for when they found a clue. Megan glanced around observing the other teams.

"I don't think the others have figured it out yet. They are all still staring at the trees," Megan noted.

"Okay, good. Let's do this!" Tasha exclaimed. Hazel had once again taken the paper with the clue and was staring at it intently. Tasha, Megan, and I all burst out laughing.

"Find anything?" Megan teased.

Hazel looked up, just realizing that everyone was staring at her.

"Oh sorry, oops," she laughed. "Here, look. *I keep the pests away, find me in the bay.*"
"I didn't understand the first clue, but I think the bay part has something to do with the pool," Hazel said.

"Good job!" Megan cheered.

We passed the junipers enclosing the patio. Then we walked by the play structure until we reached the pool.

"I'll go in!" Tasha volunteered. Still in her bathing suit from the diving contest, Tasha jumped in.

"Can I borrow someone's goggles? Sorry, I forgot mine."

"Here," I said, reaching into the clue bag where I had also put my goggles.

She quickly grabbed them and placed them over her head, making a slight adjustment.

"Thanks!" she replied, right before diving under.

We followed her shadow as we saw her swimming around. It took her a couple minutes to find the location of the clue. Then we noticed her going towards the filter vent. As she was retrieving the clue, Adam's group came sprinting toward us.

"You found the first one too?" Megan asked.

"Of course, anybody with a brain could," Adam snapped.

"Now where is that clue?" he demanded.

# CHAPTER 3:
## The Competition Begins

At that moment, Tasha resurfaced. Adam looked at her for a moment but then plastered a grin on his face.

"Do you need help getting out?" he said, his voice syrupy.

He extended his arm, and Tasha grabbed onto the other end. His smile vanished, and a sneer replaced it. He quickly grabbed the clue, which had a bottle of bug spray attached to it and pushed her back into the pool.

"Hey!" Tasha cried as she fell back into the water.

"See you later, losers!" he smirked, running off.

I helped Tasha resurface, and I realized she was crying. Tears fell off her face like a waterfall, mingling with the pool water.

"Sorry guys, I just ruined our chance of winning," she sniffed.

"That's not true, there are still three clues left," I exclaimed.

"Well, now they have a head start because I was dumb enough to trust him. I fell right into his trap."

"That could've happened to anyone; besides, the longer we keep discussing the situation, the more of a lead he has. C'mon, let's go back into that pool and grab another clue!"

"Ok," Tasha replied, now smiling through her tears.

She quickly dove back in; and, in a couple of seconds, resurfaced with the next clue. Handing it to Hazel, Tasha climbed out of the pool.

"Do you need a towel?" I asked.

"No, I think it's warm enough that I don't need it," she replied.

"Guys, hurry up," Megan said urgently. "We need to find out what this clue means before the others. They may be big and mean, but they're not the brightest. So let's figure out what this clue means and win!"

We all burst out laughing. Megan was the most competitive of all of us, so when it came to winning, she was all business.

*'Find me where sights grow clearer and objects grow larger,'* Hazel read.

"Hmm, maybe... a magnifying glass?" Megan thought aloud.

"Where would we find that?" Tasha asked.
"Yeah, there isn't really a place to put it," I said.

Meanwhile, we noticed that Hazel was now observing our surroundings.

"Magnifying glass, magnifying glass, magnifying glass...," Hazel kept muttering.

"What about it?" Megan asked excitedly.
Ignoring Megan, Hazel kept thinking.
"Magnifying glass, telescope, scope, scope... periscope!" she exclaimed.

"Huh? Can you repeat your thinking process?" Megan asked.

"Well, a magnifying glass is similar to a telescope, so I was thinking what might be in a backyard," Hazel explained.

"And?"

"A periscope!" Hazel repeated.

"You know that none of us know what that is," Megan laughed, gesturing towards our blank faces.

"It is like, well, you know those things that are attached to a submarine? Like, where you can look through something in the submarine, but the opening is above water so that you can see where you are?"

"Sort of..."

"Okay, you'll get it when you see it. Let's go!"

Following Hazel, we passed the patio and went towards the play structure.
 "I don't see Adam," Tasha pointed out.

"Well, it is a pretty big backyard, so they might be on the other side," I said.

Hazel grabbed the rope ladder attached to the play structure, and we followed her up to the second floor landing. Just as Hazel described, there was a periscope that curved out to the top.

"It looks like a J," Megan said.

"Now do you get what I mean?" Hazel asked.

"I guess," Megan replied, inspecting the outside of the periscope.

"Why don't you try looking inside it? That's a more likely spot to hide something," Hazel said.

"Oh yeah, I was going to do that," Megan mumbled, turning bright red. She peered inside and reached inside.

"Hurry up! The suspense is killing me. Are we right?" I asked.

"Yeah, sorry, it's just that it is hard to reach. I think there are a bunch of them in there. Probably one for every group."

"Just pick the first one. C'mon, we don't have all day!" Tasha said, also impatient.

"Okay, okay." She pulled out a bag with a bright blue flashlight and another slip of paper.
Hazel grabbed the bag and immediately went for the clue.

"Hey, no need to be *that* excited," Megan smiled. We grouped around Hazel and read the new clue.

*'One prize left to hunt; only the first group will find it in the front.'*

"Okaaaaay, the first part obviously means that we only have one more prize. But what does *only the first group will find it in the front* mean?" Tasha asked.

"Oh, I think I get it. Well, maybe," Hazel thought aloud.

"And?" Megan coaxed.

"Well, *front* may mean the front of the house. *First group* may mean the first group to get there."

"So, it's basically a race," Megan clarified.

"Yeah."

"Then c'mon, let's go hurry and get it!" Tasha exclaimed.

"Where even is the front?" I asked. "This place is so big, it could be anywhere!"

"Oh, I think I remember it being by the pool chairs," Megan remembered.

We rounded the play structure, and then we walked towards the pool. We crossed over to the pool chairs and went around the side of the house towards the front.

"Where do you think the clue could be?" Tasha asked.

"Hazel said the front, so why don't we go to the front of the front side?" I thought aloud.

"Huh?" the others asked, confused.

"The porch!"

"Oh yeah, that makes sense, hurry up. Let's go quickly though. If we don't rush, Adam might get there first," Megan said, starting to run.

We chased her as she went towards the porch. We were only a couple seconds behind, but we already found her looking at a slip of paper.

"Yay! You found it!" Hazel cheered. "What does it say?"

*'You have found the final prize! Good job! Please meet Ms. Starr, if you can find her!'*

"Seriously?" I groaned. "You would think that they were finally done with clues. At least we know that this is the last one."

"Yeah, but what does it mean when the clue says *'Please meet Ms. Starr, if you can find her!'*?Tasha asked.

"I think that it is still a race, so we have to beat Adam's team to find Ms. Starr," Hazel explained.

"Okay, what's the prize we got for this clue?" I inquired.
"I didn't see a prize in the bag," Megan said, worriedly.

"That's okay. Maybe there isn't a prize for this clue," I said.

"Oh yeah, okay," Megan replied, sounding relieved.

"Wait, what's that?" Hazel asked, motioning towards a bin that was behind Megan.

Megan turned around and we all crowded around the bin.

She opened up the cover and we saw four backpacks. There was one of each color: blue, green, purple, and pink.

We each got our favorite color. I grabbed the purple one, Megan got blue, Hazel reached for the green one, and Tasha picked pink.

"Why are we getting backpacks?" Megan wondered.

"Hmmm, maybe there is a theme," I said as an idea formed in my head. "Wait! I think I get it."

I reached into the clue bag and brought out the tube of sunscreen, the bottle of bug spray, and the mini flashlight.

"I think it is a camp theme," I smiled.

"You know, actually, that's makes sense!" Hazel said.

 "Yeah, so what do you think the next prize will be?" Tasha asked.

"Well, if we don't get there first, there may not be a prize," Megan replied.

"Okay, then let's go!" Tasha cried.

"Wait, we need to make a plan first," Hazel said, bringing out her notebook and pen.

"Do you always carry that everywhere?" I laughed.
"Yeah, it helps me think," she grinned.

Hazel flipped to the next blank page and started scribbling something down.

"I am going to make a map of the yard, and then we will split up to find her," Hazel explained while writing.
 "Okay, that's smart. But what do we do if we find her? How do we let the others know?" Megan asked.

"I think we need to have a code or something, because if we just shout, 'I found her!', then Adam might hear."

Megan and Tasha quickly started brainstorming a code while I looked over Hazel's map.

It looked like this:

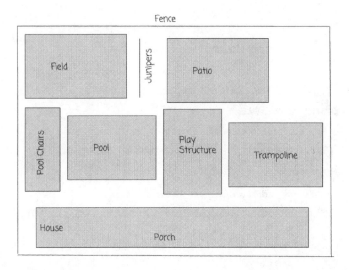

"Guys, we figured out a code," Megan announced.

"Yeah?" I asked.

"Well, we want to have something normal, but something that doesn't attract that much attention. At first, we thought of, 'Ow! My leg!', but that would attract too much attention. Then, we thought maybe something gross. Like, 'Eww, look at that _____!' But that might also make people want to see," Tasha rambled.

"Just get to the point!" Megan blurted.

"The code is to shout,' Over by the _____!'," Tasha said.

"But wouldn't that just cause everyone to go there?" I pointed out.

"Well, we are also going to flip flop everything," Mega explained.

"Here, use this," Hazel passed her notebook to Megan.

We grouped around Megan as she wrote the key.

Pool= Patio
Play Structure= House
Trampoline= Field


"This is the key, and it also works backwards, like Pool is Patio, and Patio is pool. Got it?"

We spent a couple minutes reviewing the code, and then we split up.

# CHAPTER 4:
## The Race

Tasha and I left the porch and went around the left side of the house towards the pool. We passed the pool and then went back to the playground. Other groups were crowded around the top landing.

"They must have figured out the pool clue," I thought. "We have to hurry if we want to get the final prize." Tasha seemed to be thinking the same thing, because she grabbed my arm and raced towards the play structure.

"Come one, we need to quickly figure this out or we might lose!" she whispered as we ran past the other groups.

"What exactly should we look for?" I asked.
"Well, umm, what was the clue again?"

*'You have found the final prize! Good job! Please meet Ms. Starr, if you can find her!'* I remembered.

"So I guess we just find her...?" Tasha wondered.

"Yeah, apparently so."

We split up; I went to the left side of the structure, and Tasha had the right. I started by going to the right side of the landing where Tasha stayed on the ground. I wasn't quite sure what I was looking for; either another clue about Ms. Starr, some other thing, or maybe even Ms. Starr herself.

I searched literally every crack but came up empty handed. Shoulders sagged with disappointment; I went to go check the bottom. Nothing looked out of the ordinary, and I probably would've found something in the grass because of the color contrast.

*'Hmm, maybe there is a clue in the grass. If they make it the same color of the grass, it would act like camouflage,'* I thought.

However, after searching the grass for a while, I realized that there wasn't anything out of ordinary, there weren't even any bugs except some flies.

Giving up, I started looking for Tasha. I bumped into her on the right side of the landing.

"Hey, find anything good?" I asked.

"Nope," she replied, squashing the last bit of hope I had. Noticing me facial expression, her face also turned glum.

"Okay," I sighed. "Let's try the trampoline."

We went to the left of the play structure and took a pathway that lead straight ahead. The trail leads into a small area with trees surrounding one side of the trampoline.

We stuck together this time. We first searched the right and left side, but didn't try to go to the back yet because it was covered with trees. When there was nothing on the sides, we tried the area by the trees.

"*She could easily hide here*," I realized. "*But that would be the most obvious hiding spot.*"

Tasha clearly wasn't on the same page as me as she said, "Ms. Starr is probably behind the trees!"

"Okay, umm..., why don't you check there, I am going to check underneath the trampoline."

The trampoline was at least three to four feet off the ground. Also, most trampolines are usually see-through, so you can see beneath. However, this trampoline had a cover so I wasn't able to see through it.

I ducked under and crouched to keep my head from tucking the top. I crawled towards the trees, and sure enough, I found Ms. Starr waiting on a picnic blanket with a basket in her hand.

"What the... is the final prize a picnic with you?" I asked, unable to hide my disappointment.

"Why, is that not good enough?" Ms. Starr said.

However, when she saw the look on my face, she said, "Never mind, I was just joking. I can't tell you the real prize until you bring your whole group here. You are in a group with Hazel, Tasha, and Megan, right?"

Nodding, I crawled back from underneath the trampoline. I pulled out a little note, on which I had copied Megan's key.

Pool= Patio
Play Structure= House
Trampoline= Field

"Guys, I found something by the field!" I shouted. At first, I heard nothing. Then, I heard the crunching of leaves and saw Tasha emerge from a bush.

"Hey, you found her?"

"Yep!" I replied, grinning.
Smiling back, she reached out and gave me a high five.

"Are the others coming?" she asked.

"I'm not sure; I don't think they heard me."

"Okay, let's do it together, on the count of three. One... Two... Three."

"WE FOUND SOMETHING BY THE FIELD SO HURRY UP!" we screamed at the top of our lungs.

We waited in silence for the first couple minutes, eagerly looking around. After no one came, we sat down to regain our breath.

"Do you think they heard us?" Tasha asked, a hint of annoyance had crept into her voice.

"I'm not sure, why don't we give them some time? This yard is really big; it may take some time for them to find us."

"Okay, sure, whatever."

"Fine, how about if they don't come in two to three minutes, we try and yell for them again."

"We're wasting valuable time here! The other groups may have figured out the clue."

"Do you really think Adam can figure out these clues, he doesn't even know what one plus one is!" I shouted.

I guess I had a look of absolute confidence in my face, because Tasha finally relented.

"Okay, okay. I'll wait... but only for three minutes!"

"Deal," I smiled.

We waited in silence, scanning the area to look for Hazel and Megan. Every so often, we would here a stick crack and we would both jump up in surprise.

One time, Tasha whipped her head to one side so fast that I thought she broke her neck. Obviously, I also thought she found something, so I turned in that direction. However, when I didn't see anything, I turned to Tasha.

"Did you see anything?"

"Nope, you?"

"None. It's only been a minute, so they may still be coming."

I counted thirty seconds before I saw Megan and Hazel running towards us.

Before I could say anything, Tasha yelled, "Finally! You're here!"

"Yeah! Did you find her?" Megan asked excitedly.

"Yes! Wait hold on, did you have any trouble finding us?" I said, worried.

"Nope, literally everyone ran to the field. It just took a little to find what the field meant," Megan replied.

Grabbing Hazel's notebook, she said, "There is so much stuff in here, I'm surprised it doesn't burst."

"Okay, well, let's go find out what the prize is!" Tasha cheered.

The others followed me as we dashed back to the trampoline.

"You're going to have to duck. She is underneath the trampoline," I explained.

We crawled under it and saw Ms. Starr. She waved us over.

"Hello girls, how did you like this scavenger hunt?" she asked.

"It was fun," I said. "We totally messed up on the first one."

"Yeah," the others replied, laughing.

"So, do you want to know what the prize is?"
"YES!" Megan shouted.

Hazel, Tasha, and I all burst out laughing. Ms. Starr reached into her picnic basket and pulled out four brochures and four slips of paper.

"These are camp tickets to four different camps. Here are some brochures for more information," she explained while setting them on the ground.

I looked at the different titles. One had a picture of a soccer ball. It said, "Skills and Strategies". Another brochure looked like a cookbook. That one said, "Bon Appétit!" The third brochure had a bunch of chemistry equipment on the front. It said, "Science Camp- An explosion of learning!"

The one that caught my attention the most was the last one. It had several pictures of kids doing outdoor activities, like rock climbing, swimming, canoeing, and so on. The title was, "Camp Adventuras".

"Hey, do you guys know what camp you want?" Megan asked.

"I might want the science camp if that's okay. Does anyone want it?"
When everybody shook their head, Hazel took the ticket and the brochure.

"Does anybody want the soccer camp?" Megan asked.

"No, I sort of want the adventure camp," I said.

"Okay, then I'll take the cooking camp," Tasha declared.

After grabbing our individual tickets and brochures, we thanked Ms. Starr.

"Wait, I almost forgot!" she said, beckoning for us to stay.

She pulled out three other tubes of sunscreen, three bottles of bug spray, and three different colored flashlights.

"Do you have the prizes that you collected with the clue?"

Nodding, I pulled them out of the prize bag. Now, we had four of every object.

"You can each have one of every object to use at camp. Why don't you put them in your backpack?"

I took one of each item and shoved it into my backpack. The other girls did the same.

"Thank you Ms. Starr!" we chorused.

"You're welcome. Congratulations and have fun girls!"

# CHAPTER 5:
## Camp Adventuras

"Hey Mom, remember how I won a ticket to Camp Adventuras from the scavenger hunt? Can I go? The brochure says it starts on June 15th. It's an overnight adventure camp, and I really want to go. Do you think I will be able to go? Can I, please?" I asked eagerly.

"Sure Stacy, of course you can go," Mom replied. I ran from the kitchen into my room. Glancing at my calendar, I realized it was only May 28. Oh man! Still 18 more days.

The next 18 days went by at a snail's pace. I was distracted every day by my thoughts about what might happen at camp. Both good and bad. Like meeting new friends, having bad nightmares, swimming in the big pool, getting really homesick, roasting tasty marshmallows, getting attacked by scary animals, and telling ghost stories by the campfire.

When the day finally arrived, I was so excited I thought I was going to explode! After my mom dropped me off at camp, I met Camp Director Steve. He assigned me to Bunk Number 8.

As I set up my bed, a tall girl with pale blond hair came up and said hello. She had a camp T-shirt with "Lizzy" stitched into it. The T-shirt looked 100 years old, but I didn't want to be rude so I didn't say anything.

"Hi I'm Lizzy. I've been coming to this camp for years. I can show you around, and we can be friends."

"Hi, I'm Stacy. That sounds great!" I replied, relieved that someone was willing to be my friend so quickly.

Over the next few days, Lizzy and I were basically Siamese twins joined at the hip. We ate together, signed up for the same activities, and spent all our free time together. Lizzy knew everything about the camp like the back of her hand. She always made me laugh, and we became best friends.

We were having so much fun together; we decided to ignore most of the other girls because Lizzy said they were mean, snooty and didn't deserve our attention. In addition to keeping me away from the other girls, Lizzy also had an amazing ability to make me do things I would've never done on my own.

# CHAPTER 6:
## Peanuts

One day, Lizzy came up to me and asked, "Hey Stacy, do you want to see something funny?"

"Sure, like what?" I responded. Lizzy gave me a look that told me she had something up her sleeve.

"Do you have any peanuts?" Lizzy said.

My mom was worried that I might get hungry, so she had packed nuts in my bag. She didn't know that we shouldn't bring nuts, and I wasn't sure if I should tell Lizzy about them.

I felt like something was wrong, but I just said, "Yeah, there are some in my backpack. Let's go get them!"

We ran back to our bunk and fished through my backpack until we found the peanuts.

"Watch and learn!" Lizzy exclaimed.

We ran back to the cafeteria and hid behind a table. "What are you going to do?" I whispered to Lizzy.

"Shh. Just watch."

I stayed behind the table and watched as Lizzy dashed to the nut-free tables. She raced over to one side of the table and sprinkled peanuts on the seat next to a girl named Hannah. Lizzy ran back to me and watched as Hannah screamed and jumped out of her seat.

"Peanuts! Peanuts!" Hannah shouted. Everyone else at the table also leaped out of their seats. Someone who wasn't allergic to peanuts ran over to the table to help clean the peanuts. A couple others helped pick up the peanuts before the people with allergies could actually get hurt.

"I can't believe someone would try and do this!" a boy yelled. A teacher came into the lunch area and saw the peanuts.

"Who did this?" she asked. I wasn't sure what to do! Lizzy was my friend but what she did wasn't wrong. Lizzy me gave me a look that told me to keep my mouth shut, so I did.

"WHO did this?" the teacher repeated.

No one said anything, so the teacher said, "When you feel like telling me, come find me. For now, lunch is over. Go to the pool and get ready for swimming."

Everybody rushed back to their bunks to grab their swim suits. Lizzy and I ran to the pool and got in a line behind the lifeguard. I thought of telling a teacher about what Lizzy had done, but I found I couldn't. Lizzy was my only friend at camp, and I needed to be loyal to her. So, I didn't say anything.

# CHAPTER 7:
## Swimming

"Who knows how to swim?" the lifeguard asked. The majority of the campers raised their hands.

"If you don't, please go to the grass over there," he pointed. "If you do know how to swim, then you can go jump in. Have fun!"

Lizzy and I ran to the deep end and cannonballed in. We saw a boy in the shallow end who was barely able to swim. He would doggy paddle for a little and then reach for the edge of the pool and stand. He kept doing that over and over again until Lizzy motioned for me to follow her. We went over to the boy.

"Hey, what's your name?" Lizzy asked.

"My name's Mac," he said.

"Do you want to try swimming in the deep end? You can swim really well, so I bet you can go into the deep end!"

"I'm not sur- "

"Come on!" Lizzy exclaimed, not waiting for an answer. She reached out and grabbed his hand. After helping him out of the pool, Lizzy, Mac, and I walked over to the deep end. I jumped in and treaded water. Mac and Lizzy stood at the end of the pool and looked in. I moved aside for him to enter. I had no idea what Lizzy was going to do, so I didn't say anything.

Out of the blue, Lizzy pushed Mac! As he fell, he screamed. He was still screaming when he was underwater. Lizzy reached for me and helped me out of the pool. I snatched my towel and followed her back indoors. We hid in a supply closet and listened to all the frantic cries. Lizzy laughed like crazy, and I couldn't help giggle a little at his shocked expression when he fell.

When we heard silence, we got out of the supply closet and went back to the pool. No one was there, so we picked up our stuff and went to our bunk, where we got dressed. We headed to the cafeteria where everyone was eating dinner. We joined them as if nothing had happened. After dinner, we went back to our bunk to get into our PJs. We went to the campfire and roasted marshmallows. Mac was nowhere to be seen.

"Do you know where Mac is?" I asked the girl on my left.

"He went to the camp nurse with the lifeguard," she replied. I stared at the flames wondering if Lizzy was actually a nice person. I kept thinking about that as we went to bed.

# PART II: LIZZY

## CHAPTER 8:
### Leaving Camp

The rest of the week was prank free, and I started to be super nice to everyone. Mac remained missing, and everyone speculated that he went home. I felt mad at Stacy because I could tell she was mad at me. I forgave her when she started to be nice to me again.

When it was time to leave camp, I said goodbye to Stacy and exchanged contact info so we could stay in touch. As Stacy left, I secretly followed her until she departed the campground. I remembered what my mother had said. "Remember, whatever you do, do not leave the campground or else you will be in your ghost form."

I took a risk and followed Stacy.

I drifted after her until she reached her car. She got in the front seat next to her mom. While the door was open, I flew through her into the back seat. I sat down and fell asleep as Stacy's mom drove back to wherever home was.

I woke up to the sound of someone honking. I looked around and saw that we were now driving into Stacy's garage. We were finally at her house.

I followed her wherever she went over the next month. During that time, I was able to learn some things about Stacy like her favorite things to eat at dinner and her favorite position to sleep in.

# CHAPTER 9:
## Middle School

Finally, it was time for Stacy to start school. I drifted after her while she biked. When she arrived at Acorn Middle School, she locked her bike. While she was bent over, I attached a Ghost Magnet. A Ghost Magnet was something that allowed me to follow Stacy wherever she went. I wouldn't have to fly after her. Instead, she would "pull" me.

I sat on a little bit of air and followed Stacy all about. One time, I accidently went in front of her. I got a look at her face, and I felt myself shivering with rage. She looked so much like her grandmother. Years before, Sophia (Stacy's grandmother) and I got into a little (maybe huge) argument. Since then, I had been waiting for any of Sophia's family to join me at camp.

Thirty years ago, I had tried to get Stacy's mom, Sadie, to come to camp, but she was much more excited to do other things. She was not interested in going to a fun camp and doing fun things. So I tried harder to get Stacy to go.

I also kind of brainwashed her friends and teacher to make sure she would get the adventure camp ticket. Then, I manipulated her so she would be really excited to go.

I'm sorry, but hey, it worked! She went to camp, and now I was going to get my revenge.

I followed her to her first class and then to the second. While she was getting her books from her locker, I shoved her into it and then quickly pulled off my Ghost Magnet. Her lock was still set so I was able to trap her inside. Then, I darted away from her locker as fast as I could and flew into someone else's.

I drifted down the row of lockers and into the one next to her. My plan was to pretend that I was some angel from heaven or something and save her. That way, she would be nice to me, and I could figure out what she was scared of and get my revenge. I took a deep breath and flew into her locker.

I made myself slightly visible but still looking like a ghost. I drifted toward her face and said in my best angel voice, "Hello Stacy, are you okay?"

"Who said that? " Stacy asked, whipping her head around to face me. Her eyes widened as she saw me. "Lizzy?" she wondered.

"No, I am an angel," I said. "To you, I may look like Lizzy but I look like whoever you miss most."

"Oh ok, can you help me get out of here? Somehow I fell in and the locker door closed in on me," Stacy asked.

"*Huh, so that was what she thought happened,*" I told myself.

"Of course, just give me your locker combination."

"Ok, my locker combination is 3546," Stacy responded. I flew to the other side of her locker and opened the lock. I also changed her combination to 7890. I opened the door and Stacy tumbled out. I reached for her hand to help her up, but I purposely made myself transparent, so she would fall right out of my hands.

Wham! She fell again. I had to bite my tongue to keep from bursting out laughing.

"I am so sorry!" I lied. "I forgot I was transparent."

"It's okay," Stacy said, getting to her feet. "I want to know a little more about you. Come!" She tried to grab my hand, but her hand just fell through mine. I actually thought it was funny, so I burst out laughing. I remembered that I wasn't here to have fun, I was on a mission.

I immediately stopped laughing and followed her. "*Perfect!*" I thought. "*Now I can ask her what she was afraid of.*" We talked for a little while, and I played along as an angel.

I finally asked her, "What are you afraid of?"
"Me? Oh, why?" Stacy gave me a look.

"Oh I dunno, just wondering. It's okay if you don't want to tell me." I instantly wanted to scream at myself. Why did I say that? Now I might never be able to figure out what she's afraid of.

"It's okay, I'm afraid of lions and eating old food."

"Oh." I didn't know what else to say. I was excited. Now I could start plotting my revenge.

I followed Stacy to her next class, which happened to be science.

"Hello class! Today we will start a new unit on ecosystems," Ms. Starr announced. "First, we will be going to the zoo! There we will study different animals and their homes. Animals like lions--"

When she heard this, Stacy shuddered. Suddenly, a plan formed in my brain. I was so excited to go to the zoo that I barely heard what the teacher was saying until she said that we would be going next week. She then handed out field trip forms. While she did that, I reattached my Ghost Magnet onto Stacy. I followed Stacy until the end of the day and for several days after.

# CHAPTER 10:
## The Field Trip

During the night before the science field trip, I decided to get ready. I flew out from under Stacy's bed and stole one of her backpacks. Good thing any inanimate object I touch also becomes invisible.

I drifted to the kitchen and got a water bottle as well as a hunk of buffalo meat. Stacy's mom believed that buffalo meat was more nutritious than normal beef and cooked it on Buffalo Wednesday. I put them in my backpack and found a rope in the garage. After packing the backpack, I went back to Stacy's room and fell asleep under her bed.

I felt a tug as I woke up. My Ghost Magnet was telling me that Stacy was not in her bedroom anymore. I activated my magnet, and I automatically flew to the zoo. Stacy was standing beside the elephant exhibit with her group, which included another girl and three boys. Their chaperone was trying to get the boys' attention.

"Guys, Ms. Starr wants you to head over towards the lion exhibit in five minutes. We have to go now! The exhibit is on the other side of the zoo. Come on, the lion is waiting.

When Stacy heard this, she freaked.
"Please no! No lions. I'll stay here. You can come find me here when you're done."

Unfortunately, the boys in her group were busy bickering about how cool the lion was going to be, so Stacy's chaperone didn't hear her. Her group started walking towards the lion exhibit.

I could tell Stacy wanted to stay at the elephant exhibit because she said, "Bye bye elephants. Wish me luck. I'll need it. I definitely don't want to embarrass myself."

With that, she trudged over to her group and followed them to the lion exhibit. I activated my Ghost Magnet to follow Stacy. I flew up behind her, and I listened to what Ms. Starr was saying.

"Class, what do you notice about the lion's habitat compared to the elephant's habitat?"

Stacy leaned over the rope to get a better look through the glass. As she did, an idea suddenly came to me. I transported myself past the glass enclosure so the lion could hear me.

"Lion, I have a task for you. Can you please go over to the glass wall and scare the girl?"

"Which girl? There are many of them," the lion replied.

"The one with the long ponytail and the pink shirt."

"Ok. But, why should I listen to you? Something tells me you're up to no good."

I pulled the buffalo meat out of the backpack. "If you do your job, I will give you this," I said, thrusting the meat in front of the Lion's face.

"We have a deal," the lion replied licking his lips while staring hungrily at the meat. I set the meat next to a plant and flew back to the class. I nodded at the lion, and he charged!

He ran straight up to Stacy and roared. Stacy screamed and fell back on the rope. Her head hit the floor hard, and she fainted. The rest of the class was still occupied with the lion so no one saw Stacy.

I flew over to Stacy in a rush. As I hovered beside her, a feeling that I never experienced before came over me. I shrugged it off and flew back a little as Ms. Starr came running towards us.

"Everybody, stand back," Ms. Starr said, motioning to everybody to follow her instructions. Picking two kids from the class, she then asked them to get help.

A few minutes later, they came running back with a zookeeper.

"What happened?" the zookeeper asked. "I think the lion scared her," Ms. Starr answered.

Glaring at the lion, the zookeeper said, "Bad boy, bad lion."

The lion was too busy eating his meat to notice the zookeeper's scolding.

The zookeeper introduced herself as Annelise. She and Ms. Starr kneeled next to Stacy. Suddenly, Stacy's eyelids fluttered open.

"Wh-wh-what happened?" she stuttered.

"Jason was being a bad lion, "Annelise replied.

"The Lion's name is Jason?" Stacy asked.

"Yes."

"Oh. Is, is Jason gone now?"

"Yes, you're okay. It looks like someone gave him some buffalo meat, so he won't be bothering anyone."

After visiting some of the "safer" animals, the school bus came to take the class back to their houses. On the bus ride home, Stacy rested her head until her headache disappeared. As I watched Stacy, I suddenly realized what the unfamiliar feeling was: Regret.

# CHAPTER 11:
## More Trouble

As soon as I flew into the house, I knew something was wrong. Apparently, Stacy did too because she noticed that the kitchen was a mess, and her mom usually kept the kitchen very neat. Dishes were piled in the sink, wrappers were left on the counter, and utensils were all over the place.

Stacy quickly straightened things up before going into her mother's room. She then asked, "Mom, is everything alright?"

Through tears, her mother replied, "My boss told me the company needed to cut back so I got laid off."

Stacy rushed over to her mom and sat beside her on the bed. "Oh no, are you ok? What are we going to do?"

Putting her head between her hands, her mother cried, "I have no idea." Tears trickled down her cheeks before falling into a long steady stream.

"I probably should start looking for a new job. When your father passed away, he left me some papers with some job ideas. I guess I can look through those again."

I felt a tug in the place where my heart should be. When I looked down, I saw a small patch of red, thumping like a tiny heart.

"*That's strange*," I thought. I then noticed that I started to feel yet another strange, unfamiliar feeling. As I watched Stacy hug her mother, I felt the feeling increase, but I still couldn't quite put my finger on what it might be.

Stacy's mom then trudged over to her nightstand and shuffled through some papers. She pulled out her phone and said, "Well Stacy, this might take a while. I am going call some different people to ask for job interviews."

Stacy gave her mom one last hug and left the room. I stayed behind a little and watched her mom cry a little longer, and I suddenly realized that the feeling was: Sympathy.

# Chapter 12:
# Adam

The following Monday, Stacy rode her bike to school. I rested on a puff of air trailing behind her with my Ghost Magnet. We entered the school building and looked around. Stacy noticed her friend Tasha sitting by her locker reading a book.

"Hey Tasha!" she exclaimed. Tasha looked up to see Stacy walking towards her.

"Hey, how was your weekend?" Tasha asked.

"Terrible, my mom lost her job."

"Oh, that *is* terrible, I am so so so so so sorry."

"That's ok; she is looking for a new one. I think she has 3 interviews today."

 "Yay! I hope she gets a job soon."

"Me too."

"Are you going to Megan's birthday party?"

Stacy's eyes suddenly welled up with tears. "Shoot, I don't think I can. I am not allowed to spend my money anymore, and I don't think I will be able to get a birthday present for her."

Stacy said, "I HATE that my mom lost her job. It's just so frustrating." Suddenly, Adam and his gang walked down the hall.

"Uh oh, the bullies are coming," Tasha whimpered.

"DID I HEAR SOMEONE LOST THEIR JOB???" Adam shouted in his loud screechy voice. Stacy and Tasha looked at each other.

"Uh oh, what do we do now?" Tasha whispered.

Stacy's eyes were wide with panic and she stood frozen as a statue. "I don't know!" she whisper-shouted.

57

"Here, let's just pretend that we don't have a clue what's going on. Pick up your books and we'll slide right by them, just act super casual."

"Ok, it's worth a try." Stacy gathered up her books and I stood up on my puff of air. As we strolled towards the bullies, I felt another pang. I looked down and saw the red spot swell in my chest.

"*Ewww, what in the world is going on?*" I gasped. Forgetting that others could still hear me, I clamped my mouth shut. "*Uh oh,*" I thought.

Stacy stopped and whipped her head around at the sound of my voice. "Hello? Who said that?" she called. She looked straight in my eyes for a second, and I stood frozen.
"*Does she know I'm here?*" I thought.

"Lizzy?" she asked. "Is that you?"

"*How does she see me?*" I wondered. "*Yikes, uh oh.*"

"No, I must be seeing things," Stacy thought aloud. She shut her eyes and shook her head as if trying to clear her vision. I took that chance to fly above her, so that when she looked around, she couldn't see me unless she looked up.

She re-opened her eyes, and when she didn't see me, she shook her head.

"Yeah, I must be seeing things," she confirmed.

"Shhh, they're getting closer," Tasha said.

We continued walking, and I braced myself. As much as I resented Stacy, I felt badly for her. At that moment, Adam made eye contact with Stacy. His mouth opened like he was going to say a rude comment, but then his gaze landed exactly to my eyes. Mouth gaping he stared at me for a second before shaking his head. He then turned around and ran down the same way he came.

"That was weird," Tasha said, breaking the silence.

Something tickled the edge of my brain, like there was something I needed to know but kept forgetting. Intrigued, I unlatched my Ghost Magnet and flew down the way Adam left.

I flew up a little farther, and saw him standing alone shaking his head like something was wrong. He turned around just as I came up to him. His skin tone paled noticeably, and he whispered uncertainly, "Hello, is anybody there?"

Finally, I understood. Evil was able to see ghosts. If someone had a twisted, unpure soul, they were able to see other twisted souls. I guess that after all his bullying, he was considered "evil".

"I'm Lizzy," I informed him. "You're Adam, right?"

"How did you know that?" he asked, his skin looked even paler if that was possible.
"I know things," I smiled.

"What do you want?" he trembled.

"Good question, except I came here to ask *you* that."

"Umm, well, it... I... umm.. so... I guess I'm known for wanting to tease people. But these days, everyone takes things too seriously so they are all scared of me and, umm, I've just always wanted to take revenge on Stacy since her group beat mine during the scavenger hunt," he said sheepishly.

"Oh, it looks like we're on the same page! I'm a ghost who is trying to get Stacy back for something her relatives did to me," I replied casually, like it was perfectly normal for me to go around telling everyone that I was a ghost.

His mouth dropped to the ground. Eyes wide and mouth gaping, he stuttered, "You're a-a-a g-gh-ghost?"

"Yeah, do you have a problem with that?" I said, stiffly.

Some of his old composure returned as he smiled. "No, not at all. Sorry to offend you."

"Okay, thanks," I smiled.

"Then let's team up," he said slyly.

# CHAPTER 13:
## Change of Heart

The next day at school, I immediately unhooked myself from the Ghost Magnet and flew to find Adam. I cornered him on his way to history. He glanced in my direction and did a double take.

Quickly getting over his surprise, he motioned me to follow him. I drifted along as he guided me towards an empty hallway. We paused at a door with a plaque that read "Mr. Johnson's Janitor Closet".

"Why is this dude's name on a plaque?" I asked, bewildered.

"Oh, he's like some famous janitor guy for our school or something. I didn't really care so I didn't pay attention during the school tour."

"Where is this place?" I gestured towards the deserted hallway.

"I think it is where all the awards and stuff get stored away."

"Okay, cool." Refocusing on the more important matter, I asked, "So, why did you take me here?"

"Oh yeah, you wanted to tell me something? I just brought you here to talk without people bothering us."

"Yeah, I was wondering what we should do to little brat over there," I motioned to a nearby hall with Stacy's science classroom.

"Well, last night, I stayed up brainstorming ideas."

"And?" I prompted.

"Well, what if we embarrass her in front of everybody? That is one of the worst ways to humiliate someone. I was thinking we could lure her someplace and then tease her or do something."

"Smart! What if we get her to the middle of the hall? Then, we can fling stuff like rotten old food at her. She's terrified of old food."

"Yeah! I'll do the luring, and you can do the throwing. That way, she won't know who's doing it!" he laughed, looking like a little boy who just got a chest of new toys.

Grinning, he asked, "Are you in?"

Beaming back, I started to say yes. Suddenly, before I knew it, I said a word I never thought I would say.

"No."

# CHAPTER 14:
## The Transformation

Darkness swallowed me whole, and I felt like someone had ripped my life out. I was in too much pain, I couldn't think, I couldn't speak.

Finally, a burst of colors flashed before me, and I felt myself go through a wide range of emotions in a timespan of seconds: happy, sad, excited, angry, amazed, nervous, cheerful, disappointed, peppy, jealous, confident, greedy, brave, scared. Fear, so much fear, overwhelming me in a way I never thought possible.

Finally, after what felt like an eternity, the lights disappeared. However, I didn't feel normal, I felt strange. Summoning all of my energy, I used all of my strength to open my eyes. I was on the ground, on a blanket.

"Wh-whe-where a-am uh-uh-I?" I managed.
"Shh, rest," a soothing voice responded.
I heard lots of worried whispers, and they
worked themselves into my dreams.

*"What is going on?"*

*"What is wrong with her?"*

*"Is she dead?"*

However, there was one more that hurt above all
the others, one that stung like the pain all over.

*"What* is *she? How did she just...* appear*?"*

Finally, I woke up. A pair of blue eyes stared
down at me. I recognized the face, and a new
wave of worries crashed over me.

"Lizzy?" a small tentative whisper escaped from
her mouth.
"Stacy," I coughed. "I am so sorry."

"For what? What did you do?"

"How- how can you see?" I groaned.

"See? Umm, are you alright?" she asked, her
brows creased with worry.

I looked down at myself and gasped.

My skin was pale, but fleshy. I could hear my heart thumping in my chest, my blood pulsing through my body. I could see my chest rising up and down with every breath I took. I could see the other startled faces staring down at me, none of them I knew except for Stacy. I could taste the saliva in my mouth. The realization hit me like nothing else in the world.

There was only one possible answer.

I had become human.

Kelly A. Yang

## ABOUT THE AUTHOR

Kelly Yang is a 5th grade student at Bullis Charter School and an avid reader and writer. She has been published twice in the *Los Altos Town Crier* as well as the Bullis Charter School blog. She hopes to become a famous writer of action adventure stories.

In addition to writing, Kelly loves to play soccer, sing, surf, bake brownies, eat brownies and ice cream, fiddle on her viola and care for her menagerie of 10 pets.

Made in the USA
San Bernardino, CA
21 March 2020